Say please, Louise!

A cautionary tale

Phil Roxbee Cox
Illustrated by Jan McCafferty

Edited by Jenny Tyler
Designed by Non Figg

Photographic manipulation by Nick Wakeford

First published in 2007 by Usborne Publishing Ltd., 83-85 Saffron Hill, London, EC1N 8RT, England www.usborne.com

This is the tale of little Louise.

A dreadful young girl,
who would never say please.

What Louise wanted, she simply took:

a piece of toast,

a seat,

a book.

"Say please, Louise!"
the others pleaded.

"A 'please' and 'thank you'
is all that's needed."

She would never ever wait her turn,
say please or thank you.

She'd never learn.

Her poor parents were left in despair,
    but little Louise simply did not care.

"Say please, Louise!"
the others pleaded.

"A 'please' and 'thank you'
is all that's needed."

"I want some ice cream!"

"Take me to the lake!"

"Buy me a toy boat!"

"Get me some cake!"

9

"Say please, Louise!"
the others pleaded.

"A 'please' and 'thank you'
is all that's needed."

Louise would SHOUT

she would COMMAND.

She would ORDER

she would DEMAND.

"Say please, Louise!"
the others pleaded.

"A 'please' and 'thank you'
is all that's needed."

But all was to change, one Sunday at two, when her parrot escaped...

...and flew into the blue.

"I want a new pet!
I don't care what you say!
I want a new pet
and I want one TODAY!"

"Say please, Louise!"
the others pleaded.

"A 'please' and 'thank you'
is all that's needed."

The following day,
at Wilson's Pet Store,

Louise made an announcement
as she burst through the door.

"I don't want
a goldfish, snake,
lizard or bunny,

or hamster
or guinea pig,
or that frog
that looks funny.

16

I don't want the insect
with the six sticky feet,

or the canary named Mary,
or that blue parakeet."

"I don't want a dog
and I don't want a cat."

She pointed up high.
"What I want is
THAT!"

18

And do you know what her dad DIDN'T do that day?

He didn't mention manners. He simply said, "OK."

The bird studied Louise
with an unblinking eye,
grabbed her in its talons
and screeched, "Time to fly!"

Then it flapped
its huge wings
and flew up, up
and away...

...and little Louise has
not been seen to this day.

But there are those who claim to
have heard on the breeze,

a small distant voice crying out,

"help me..."

23

"...PLEEEEEEEEEEEEEEEEEASE!"